Dizzy's Walk

Malorie Blackman

Illustrated by Pamela Venus

Tamarind Ltd

Sponsored by **NASUWT**

To Neil and Elizabeth
with love

and thanks to
Jordan and his family

"Playing games again?
Now there's a surprise!
What you two need
is some exercise.

Dizzy wants to go
for a walk." said Mum.

"And don't buy any sweets and cakes
on the way or you'll spoil your lunch!

And remember to watch that naughty Dizzy."

"Dad, look at these bright shiny things. Bracelets, necklaces, watches and rings.

But I'd rather have a model spaceship any day."

"Scrumptious-delumptious!
Just smell those strawberries.
Look at those grapes and those sweet,
juicy cherries," said Jack.

"We'll get some on our way back," said Dad.

"Where's Dizzy gone?"

"Hi, Amy."
"Hello, Jack. I'm in a hurry.
I'm looking for my cat."

"Ow! A banana skin!
Who put that there?"

"Look at that spaceship," said Jack.

"You'll have to wait till Christmas," laughed Dad.

"Come down.
Dizzy's gone now,
you're safe."

"Dad, are you going to buy
Mum some flowers?
She says you never do."

"Yes, I think I will," said Dad.
"But don't tell her
you told me to!"

"Oh, no!"

"This shop sells lollies, ice-creams and sweets," said Jack.

"Is that a hint?" laughed Dad.

"Look, Dad.
Doughnuts and sandwiches,
jam tarts and cake.
Yummy and scrummy!
I love things you bake."

"Uhmmm," said the man.

"Stay
Dizzy.
Stay!"

"Keep an eye on Dizzy, Jack,"
said Dad.

"You messy pup. Get out of there!"

"Off you go Dizzy and have a good run.
We're going to sit here and guzzle a bun,"
said Jack.

"And Mum will never know!" Dad winked.

"I wonder what Dizzy's doing?"

"Don't let your dog chase my ducks!
If she does it again, I'll get really cross,"
said the park keeper.

"We'd better go home now,
it's getting quite late."

"Come on you slow coach,
let's race to the gate,"
said Jack.

"You two look exhausted!" said Mum.
"Are you ready for lunch?
And did Dizzy behave?"

"Yes, she wasn't bad once," said Dad.

"That's right, Mum," said Jack.
"We got along fine.
Dizzy was good all of the time."

OTHER TAMARIND TITLES

Marty Monster
Mum's Late
Rainbow House
Starlight
Zia the Orchestra
Jessica
Where's Gran?
Toyin Fay
Yohance and the Dinosaurs
Time for Bed
Dave and the Tooth Fairy
Kay's Birthday Numbers
Mum Can Fix It
Ben Makes a Cake
Kim's Magic Tree
Time to Get Up
Finished Being Four
ABC – I Can Be
I Don't Eat Toothpaste Anymore
Giant Hiccups
Boots for a Bridesmaid
Are We There Yet?
Kofi and the Butterflies
Abena and the Rock – Ghanaian Story
The Snowball Rent – Scottish Story
Five Things to Find –Tunisian Story
Just a Pile of Rice – Chinese Story

For older readers, ages 9 – 12
Black Profiles Series
Benjamin Zephaniah
Lord Taylor of Warwick
Dr Samantha Tross
Malorie Blackman
Baroness Patricia Scotland
Mr Jim Braithwaite

A Tamarind Book

Published by Tamarind Ltd, 1999

Text © Malorie Blackman
Illustrations © Pamela Venus
Edited by Simona Sideri

ISBN 1 870516 41 9

Designed and typeset by Judith Gordon
Printed in Singapore